Jay Grows an Alien

Jay Grows an Alien

Caroline Anne Levine

APC
Autism Asperger Publishing Co.
P.O. Box 23173
Shawnee Mission, Kansas 66283-0173
www.asperger.net

© 2007 Autism Asperger Publishing Co.
P.O. Box 23173
Shawnee Mission, Kansas 66283-0173
www.asperger.net

All rights reserved. No part of the material protected by this copyright notice may be reproduced or used in any form or by any means, electronic or mechanical, including photocopying, recording, or by any information storage and retrieval system, without the prior written permission of the copyright owner.

Publisher's Cataloging-in-Publication

Levine, Caroline Anne.

Jay grows an alien / Carline Anne Levine. -- 1st ed. -- Shawnee Mission, KS : Autism Asperger Pub. Co., 2007.

p. ; cm.

ISBN-13: 978-1-931282-29-1
ISBN-10: 1-931282-29-3
LCCN: 2006932487

1. Asperger's syndrome--Juvenile fiction. 2. Friendship--Juvenile fiction. 3. Self-esteem in children--Juvenile fiction. 4. Life on other planets--Juvenile fiction. 5. Extraterrestrial beings. I. Title.

PZ7.L57832 J39 2006
[Fic]--dc22   0611

This book is designed in Myriad and Broken.

Printed in the United States of America.

Dedication

In memory of Pat Falwell

Special thanks to: Dr. Penny Bustin, Linda Aston, Seth Goldberg, Shari Abramson, Rod Levine and Julie Wakeman-Linn.

Chapter One

THE SPACE CADET

"Oh no!" Jay said out loud as he walked into class. There was a substitute and did he smell bad. He hated it when Mrs. Kim, his regular teacher, was out.

Jay held his nose as he sat at his desk. This made his mouth hot and dry. He needed water, but the bell rang, so it was too late to get up.

The teacher had written his name on the board, Mr. Grimes. Next to it was the schedule for the day. The last activity was P.E. but Jay already knew that. It was the reason he hadn't slept well last night.

"Okay, class," Mr. Grimes said, clapping his hands, "take your seat."

Jay slid out of his chair, then picked it up. His regular teacher never gave such strange orders, but Jay always tried to do what teachers asked.

"Put it down," Drew whispered. Drew was his class buddy. He helped Jay follow the rules, but it was too late.

Hunter, a mean boy in back of Jay, whispered, "Keep holding it!" He always enjoyed seeing Jay get in trouble.

The substitute was at Jay's desk in a flash. "Do you think that's funny?" he asked.

Jay shook his head.

"Put it down," Drew whispered again.

"Then why are you holding your chair?" the substitute asked, leaning closer to Jay's face.

Jay started to gag. He ran to the door and barfed as soon as he reached the hall. In the background, he heard the kids yelling, "Eww, eww!"

Mr. Grimes came running out to him. The rest of the class stood watching at the door. "Back to your seats!" the teacher told them. Drew stayed.

"I'll take him to the nurse, Mr. Grimes."

Jay was glad to be in the Health Room with Mrs. Shelly. She was kind to him each day when he stopped by to take his pill. She wiped his face and found him a clean t-shirt.

"The sub's after-shave made me barf," Jay told her. "Perfume, perfume."

"The sub got mad at Jay for picking up his chair," Drew added, "then he came over and yelled at him. He smells like he put a whole bottle of after-shave on."

Mrs. Shelly sat down next to Jay on the cot. "I'm sorry you got sick," she said. "I know perfume really bothers you. Do you think you'd be able to work in the back of the classroom for the rest of the day?"

Jay thought a second and then nodded. He waited while Mrs. Shelley wrote a note to the sub to let him back into class.

Back in class, Jay gave the note to the sub. Instead of sitting down in their regular seats, Drew took their books and supplies to the table at the back of the room. "I don't think his after-shave will get to you back here," he said.

"It's too noisy, noisy," Jay said.

Drew went to Jay's desk, got his headset and gave it to him.

"Thanks," Jay said, putting it on. For the millionth time, Jay wished Drew was his friend. But he knew Drew was nice to him because Mrs. Kim had asked him to be his class buddy. Drew was smart like Jay, but didn't have Asperger's.

Jay turned the white noise dial to "low." That way he could still hear the teacher and Drew, while keeping the classroom noise down. It was one way he could stay calm.

After math and spelling, it was time for reading. Jay's and Drew's group was reading Aesop's fable about the fox who couldn't reach a bunch of grapes on a grapevine. Jay hadn't started his fable report at home because the story confused him. He knew it wasn't just about the fox so he had read it again. If only it were about outer space or dogs, *real* outer space or dogs. He didn't like make-believe stories.

"Jay," the sub asked, "why did the fox say the grapes were sour?"

"I was wondering about that too," Jay said, scratching his ear and looking past the teacher.

Everyone laughed except the teacher. "You think you're really funny, don't you?"

"No," Jay answered, frowning.

"Then why did you give me that answer?"

"Because I don't understand about the fox," Jay replied. "Since he couldn't reach the grapes, he wouldn't know if they were sour or not. So why did he say they were sour?" Jay looked at the picture of the grape vine in his reader. "Oh, I know," he said in his too-loud voice, "these grapes are very light green. They probably *were* sour."

The sub stared at him. "I get it now – you're one of those space cadets." Jay heard him say under his breath, "Nice of them to let me know."

Jay's leg jiggled under the table because he was totally confused. The sub said he was a space cadet, but how could he be? He hadn't gone to any space camp where he'd learn to be a space cadet. He had begged his parents many times to send him to one, but they always said they didn't have enough money.

"Stop that banging!" the sub warned.

Jay saw Drew pointing to his leg and stopped jiggling. But soon his head had that tight, dizzy feeling. He made his hands into fists and then slowly relaxed them. He did it six times and then his head felt better. It was one of the ways Mr. Goodman, his resource teacher, had taught him to relax.

An hour later, it was finally time for lunch. Jay took his lunch bag to the cafeteria. He wished Drew had to eat with him, but that wasn't part of his duties. He only had to help him when they were in class together, not in the cafeteria or on the playground.

Jay ate at his regular table, the one closest to the door. That way, if the noise and smells made him panicky, he could get out fast and go to the Health Room. Jay was minding his own business, eating his oatmeal crackers, when something hit his face. He screamed and flapped his hands.

"Hey, Foxie, don't you like the grapes?" Hunter yelled. "They're real sweet!" He laughed in his usual mean way.

"No," Jay said and started to choke on his cracker. He heard kids yelling for the lunchroom aides.

The aides ran to help him. When they saw he was all right, they looked around to see who had thrown the grapes.

When one of the aides asked who threw the grapes, none of the kids answered. In the meantime, Hunter sat at his table eating like a perfect gentleman.

"I want to go to the Health Room," Jay said, "Health Room, Health Room." He needed to get out of there before he started to cry.

"Sure," the aide said, shaking her head. "Jay, you're so

nice, I don't know why kids treat you like this. I just wish I could catch them."

In the Health Room, Mrs. Shelly gave Jay a packet of soda crackers and a cup of water. "Only two more hours till you go home," she told him.

Jay looked at his watch. It was 1:30. He knew he would get on the bus at 3:30, and that was two hours away. But he didn't know whether that was a long time or a short time. He hoped it would be soon. Then he groaned because he remembered he still had to get through P.E. But after that, he'd be on the bus home. Home, where his sister, Kyla, would have his popcorn ready, the plain kind. Home, where Noodle, his dachshund, would cuddle with him on the bed. Home, where he would sit in front of his computer and play space games. All Jay wanted was to relax and forget this rotten day.

Chapter Two

"Where's my popcorn?" Jay asked the minute he got home.

Kyla got paid for taking care of him before and after school and for getting dinner started. Two of her jobs were to have his popcorn ready when he came home and to shop for last-minute groceries. Jay looked around the kitchen for his snack, but didn't see it.

"I'll make your popcorn after we go to Groceries and More," Kyla said as she grabbed her car keys from the little table by the back door. "I didn't have time to after school because some friends helped me with volleyball and I just got home. We have to go get some salad stuff for dinner."

He started to flap. "I don't want to shop," he said. "Popcorn, popcorn."

Kyla groaned and threw down her keys. "You can eat it in the car, then. You're such a pain in the neck."

While Jay listened to the soft pinging of the popcorn in the microwave, he wondered how his eating it in the car could give Kyla neck pain. Would she get a pain if she turned around to check on him? It never hurt his neck to turn around in the car.

"Kyla, how can I give you a pain in the neck when I'm not even touching you?"

Kyla smirked and said, "It means you're bothering me – you're nagging me to make your popcorn right this second."

Jay finished his popcorn, then remembered he needed to check in with Mom at her office. He did this every day after school.

"How's my little man?" Mom asked when he called.

"Okay," he answered. "We're going to Groceries and More. Bye."

As Jay and Kyla were getting ready to leave, Jay

remembered to put on his headset. Sometimes babies screamed in Groceries and More, and he hated that sound.

At Groceries and More, Kyla told Jay to wait for him in the toy aisle.

"You said we were going to shop for salad stuff for dinner," Jay said. He flapped his hands and added, "Dinner, dinner."

"I'll just be a few minutes, Asp-booger," she answered, "then I'll come back for you."

"But you said we were going to shop for dinner," Jay repeated. He liked toys, but hated any change in plans. This was the second plan she had broken this afternoon, and he was still feeling jumpy from his rotten day at school.

At the end of the toy aisle, Jay found a bin full of marked-down toys. The sign above it said, "Summer Sale–50-75% Off Regular Price." He leaned over the bin and looked at each toy in turn. There were fashion dolls, tea sets, cars, trucks and playing cards. Nothing was of interest to him; he was ready to give up. "Wait," he suddenly said out loud. At the bottom of the bin was a colorful piece of cardboard with some toy capsules attached. He grabbed it and ran his finger over the clear plastic bumps covering the capsules. "Magic

Grow-E-Aliens," he read. "Drop in warm water and watch a space alien come to life! $2.50." On the back someone had written "75% off."

Jay closed his eyes and did the math. "Sixty-two cents and three cents for tax," he mumbled. He looked in his coin purse and found one quarter, two dimes and three nickels. Then he started looking around the store for his sister, calling, "Kyla, Kyla, Kyla." When he finally found her, she was in the boring cosmetics aisle holding a tube of Zits-Off and Heavenly Blue eye shadow.

"Jay," she hissed, "I told you to wait for me."

Jay pointed at her Zits-Off. "You should get that," he said in his usual loud voice, "because you have lots of zits." He got close to her forehead and started to count.

Kyla clapped her hand over his mouth. "Do you have to announce it to the whole store?"

Jay pealed off Kyla's hand. He didn't like to be touched, especially on his face. "But you do have lots of zits. Can you loan me five cents?"

"Okay," she said, "I'll give you the money if you keep your trap shut."

"But I don't have a trap," he said, tapping the capsules on the back of his leg. "Traps are a mean way to catch animals, and I like animals. Can I have five cents, five cents?"

"Yeah," she said, blowing the bangs off her forehead.

Jay noticed she did this a lot when they were together, but he didn't know why.

Looking at the eye shadow in her hand, he offered, "I could organize your eye shadows when we get home. I could do them according to the colors of the rainbow, alphabetically, from lightest to darkest, or from darkest to lightest."

"Don't you dare touch my eye shadow!" Kyla yelled.

When they got home, Kyla took the capsules out of the bag and looked at them. "These have so many dents, they'll never work. You didn't use your head."

Jay scrunched his eyebrows. "Yes, I did," he said, "I figured out what 75% of ..."

"Forget it, Number-Head. That's not what I meant."

They put the groceries away together. Jay had organized the pantry a long time ago into the following categories: tomato products, pasta, cereals, baking products, canned fruit and vegetables, crackers and dog products.

After they were done, Kyla made peanut butter sandwiches for them.

"I hate that smell," Jay complained. He cut his sandwich into neat little squares and fed them to Noodle. "I want something else."

"Peanut butter is yummy," Kyla said, chewing with her mouth open. "Look, Noodle's scarfing it down."

Jay held his nose. "Eww, you're making the smell go all over the place!" He went to the pantry and found his oatmeal crackers. Everything about them was right – their taste, their smell, their color and the way they felt when he chewed them.

After that Jay helped Kyla practice volleyball. The deal was, for every hour he helped her, she had to spend an hour with him at the library. There were so many books on outer space, he needed lots of time to choose them. Jay kept track of the time in a little notebook with the moon on the cover.

"I need to practice spiking today," Kyla told him, "otherwise, I'll never make the team."

Jay tossed the ball over the net for what seemed like hours. Kyla tried to spike it just inside Jay's side of the net. Finally she hit one over.

"Good job!" he told her, picking up the ball. "Maybe you'll make the team."

"Well," Kyla said, "third time's a charm."

"Do you get a charm for trying three times?" Jay asked, wiping sweat from his forehead.

"No," Kyla answered. "It's just a saying. Means you hope you'll finally get something on your third try."

Jay wondered why she didn't say that the first time.

Later in his room, Jay hydrated five of the six toy capsules in a bucket of warm water while Noodle lay at his feet watching. In a few minutes, the capsules dissolved, and five tiny pieces of sponge floated to the top.

Jay examined a red one. It had little blobs for arms and legs and a large one for a space helmet. "Dumb," he mumbled, throwing them all the trash.

That night at dinner Dad asked about everyone's day.

"We went to the store and Jay bought some beat-up toy capsules," Kyla said.

Jay looked at his table mat and said, "Kyla bought Zits-Off for her pimples."

"You just had to say that!" she said, socking him.

"Don't hit your brother," Mom scolded.

"But Mom," Kyla said, "why's he always hurting my feelings? And why doesn't he look at people when he talks? He's so weird."

Upset, Jay ran to the family room, flapping his arms.

Noodle followed, and together they burrowed under the cushions on the sofa. Jay left his head out so he could still hear the others talking in the dining room. He wanted to know why he said stuff like that, too. He didn't think he was a mean kid.

Dad sighed. "Kyla, you know why."

Jay heard Kyla stomp her foot. "Right," she said, "because he's got asp-boogers."

"I don't like your attitude, young lady," Mom warned.

"Well," Kyla yelled, "I don't like having a weirdo brother!" Then she scraped back her chair and stomped to her room.

Jay cried into the sofa cushions. He knew he was different from other kids, but he hated being called weirdo and Asp-booger. He'd heard his parents talk about his asp-boogers after all those doctor appointments, but it never made sense. He wasn't an asp, a small poisonous snake from Egypt. And he'd read enough snake books to know that snakes didn't have boogers.

After a little while Dad came in and sat next to him. "Hot dog time?" he asked.

Jay nodded, and Dad tossed the sofa quilt onto the carpet.

"Okay, Hot Dog," Dad said, "Lie down on the bun."

Jay lay on his back, his arms and legs close to his body. "Noodle come," he said. He knew the little dachshund liked to be a hot dog, too.

Dad rolled the quilt tightly around and around them, seam side down.

"Rock us," Jay asked.

Dad rolled them back and forth until Jay said, "Woof," their signal for Dad to unroll them. "Feel better, Hot Dog?" Dad asked.

Jay nodded. He needed to answer Dad's question.

"Dad, since I'm not an asp, how can I have asp-boogers?" he asked, snuggling next to him.

Dad chuckled. "You don't have asp boogers, you have something called Asperger Syndrome. Your brain works differently and certain things are hard for you. For example, not knowing that mentioning Kyla's Zits-Off would embarrass her, and not understanding sayings like, 'it's raining cats and dogs,' and not wanting to look at people when you talk." Dad smiled and added, "And it is also why you're an expert on the solar system and why your sister calls you 'Number-Head' because you're so fast at calculating. And why you don't make a good liar."

Jay frowned. "Are those good things?"

"Very good things," Dad said.

"But Kyla said I'm a weirdo," Jay said, curling and uncurling the bottom of his shirt between his fingers. "Can't a doctor make it go away?"

Dad shook his head, "No, but there are lots of things to learn that'll make it easier for you. And as I just said, there are many parts of your Asperger's that are positive. You wouldn't want to lose them."

At bedtime Jay changed into his favorite pajamas, the soft ones with no labels inside. As he was climbing into bed with Noodle, he noticed the last capsule on his desk. "It's not very bent," he said out loud. "I'll hydrate it." Jay poured put warm water in the bucket again, dropped in the capsule and put it on his dresser to watch in bed. "Why's it taking so long, so long?" he asked Noodle.

Noodle growled and bared his teeth at the bucket.

"It's okay, Noodle," Jay told him, "it's just a toy." Noodle turned around a couple of times and then dropped next to Jay. He growled softly at the bucket until he fell asleep.

"Help me, Earth-Boy," Jay suddenly heard. Part of a dream, he thought as he dozed off.

"Help me! Help me!" This time Jay was sure he had heard a voice. He opened his eyes and looked to where the sound was coming from. Noodle stood next to him, growling in a way Jay had never heard before.

Jay stared and flapped hard. The Grow-E-Alien had grown all right! She was about his size. She was sitting on his dresser with her foot stuck in the bucket.

Chapter Three

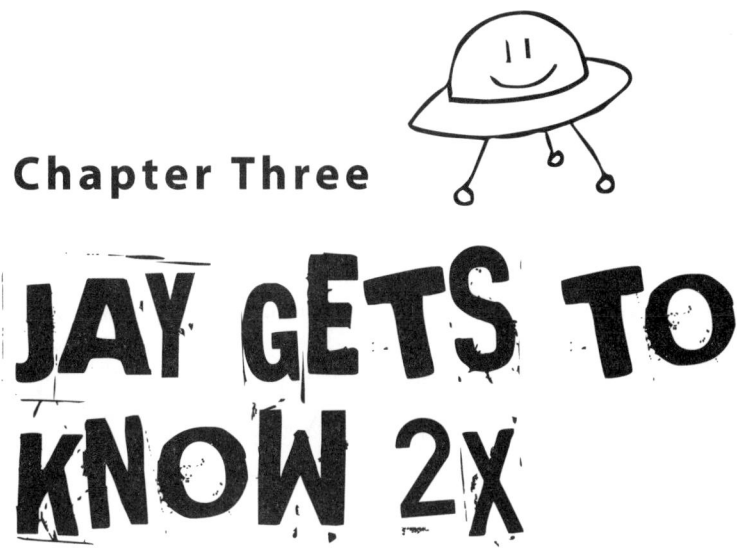

JAY GETS TO KNOW 2X

The alien pointed to the bucket. "What is this object on my foot?"

"On my foot, on my foot," Jay repeated.

"Yes, Earth-Boy," the alien said, "I do know it is on my foot. Please inform me what the object is."

"It's a bucket," Jay answered, staring at the alien. He didn't know why, but it didn't bother him to look at her eyes while they talked, the way it normally did.

"Do Earth-Kids wear buckets?" she asked. Then she pointed to Noodle. "Why is your animal making that noise?"

"No, of course we don't wear buckets," Jay told her. "And as far is the animal Noodle is concerned, he's my dog. He's growling at you because he's scared." Then he scooped Noodle up and held him tight. But Noodle kept growling and wiggled to get down.

"Your eyes are strange – the way they're looking at me," he said to the alien. "They don't blink and they hardly move. Are they sending X-rays into my head? Can you read my thoughts?"

At that the alien jumped onto Jay's bed, the bucket hitting his night stand.

"My eyes are standard cyborg eyes. They do not send X-rays. I cannot read your thoughts, but that would be an interesting activity. I will ask Dr. Eo if he can program me to do that."

Jay's eyes got big, and he started to flap again.

"Earth-Boy," she continued, "do not be afraid of me. I came here to be your friend." She put out her hand. "I will not ask for a mind-reading program."

"Good," Jay said, also putting out his hand. He remembered it was the polite thing to do. But was hers electric? Her hair was a mess of thin gold wire. Maybe it was electric, too. Maybe her whole body was electric. But when they shook hands, Jay noticed hers was tan like his. It felt soft on the outside, hard on the inside, like his toy space captain.

"I am 2X," the alien said, patting her hair. "Thank you for putting me into the bucket of warm water. It felt so good to stretch."

"Uh huh," Jay said, pointing at her other arm. It had a small computer keyboard and screen. "Does it work?"

"I am not certain of that," she said, "since I am five million light years away from my planet." Then she spoke into her arm, "On." In a kid's voice, the computer answered, "At your service."

"Wow!" Jay said, leaning close to the alien. "It's voice-activated."

2X held out her arm. "You may try it."

Jay pressed the key with the word, "Dr. Eo" because it was interesting – EO-1 was the name of N.A.S.A.'s Earth polar-orbiting satellite. Outer space was Jay's special interest. If the grown-ups would let him, he'd spend every waking minute studying it.

"2X," a man's voice said, "where on Earth are you?" Her screen showed a man with an oxygen mask.

"Cool!" Jay said, touching the screen.

"Cool," 2X repeated. "I am in Cool."

Jay giggled. "No, you're not in Cool. You're in Washington, DC, the capital of the United States. Cool means something is a little cold."

2X shook one of her long fingers at the screen. "Dr. Eo," she said, "my Very Beginning English program confuses me."

"I will send you the Ready for More English Program," Dr. Eo replied, "Please sit in the Earth's sun so I can transmit it. That is all."

"That is all; that is all," Jay repeated. "What does sitting in the sun have to do with getting your program?"

"First," she answered, "tell me why you flap and repeat what I say."

"Flap?" Jay asked, looking at his arms. "It makes me feel good. Repeat? I don't know; I just do it."

"Hey, Number-Head," Kyla yelled from downstairs, "breakfast is ready."

"Who just spoke?" 2X asked, peeking out the door.

Jay put on his slippers. "That's my sister, Kyla. She's sixteen. What's that funny noise you're making? It sounds like a growling stomach and ... a garbage disposal." He put his ear next to her middle. "I didn't think cyborgs had stomachs and garbage disposals."

"I do not know what a garbage disposal is, but I do not have one. I have a stomach, however. I am the first cyborg from Zuse to have a stomach. "Dr. Eo installed it before he dehydrated me to fit in the capsule. However, I do not growl because I am not a dog."

"A dog?" Jay asked, rubbing Noodle behind his ear. "Oh, I get it. Dogs growl, not stomachs. Is that what you mean?"

"That is correct," 2X said. "Dr. Eo told me when my stomach makes that noise I need to put food into my mouth."

Jay giggled. "You eat, so does that mean you poop?"

"What is poop?" 2X asked.

Jay laughed and pointed to her computer. "Ask it," he said. "I like you, you're funny." He opened the door. "I'll take you to the kitchen."

2X shook her head. "I cannot. Dr. Eo said, 'you can trust Earth-People who are not yet teenagers. For all the others, watch, then meet.'"

2X looked around the room and picked up one of Jay's space explorers. "This will be good," she said. She bit off its white space-helmeted head and chewed. "Oh, it is delicious!"

Jay waved his arms and yelled, "That's Captain Quasar, my best space figure. Why are you eating it?"

"My program said it was a potato, a delicious Earth-food. I am sorry." She gave Jay the headless space toy.

Then she pointed to the window shades. "Please make the Earth's sun come into this room. Doctor Eo will send my new program through your sun's rays."

"So that's how it works," Jay said, pulling up the shades. Sunlight filled his room. "2X," he asked, not waiting for her answer, "did you know the sun's energy comes from its core and its temperature is fifteen million degrees centigrade? And that it takes a million years for the sun's energy to get to Earth, so the energy to run your computer is old, but it's still good energy?" He took a deep breath and went on, "Did you know the sun is the biggest part of our solar system and ..."

"Jay!" Kyla called again, "your oatmeal's getting cold."

Jay went down to the kitchen, fed Noodle and sat down across from Kyla.

"What was all that noise?" she asked.

Jay took a teaspoon of sugar and carefully sprinkled it in rows on his oatmeal, the way he did every morning. "I was talking to a space alien," he said. "She came from my last capsule."

Kyla rolled her eyes. "Yeah right, and I just won the lottery."

Jay jerked up. "You did? How much did you win?"

"Number-Head," she said, "I didn't win anything. Just like you didn't turn a toy capsule into a space alien."

Jay picked up Noodle. "But I did," he went on. "Her name is 2X, and she took all night to hydrate from the capsule and ..."

"Put Noodle down and eat your oatmeal," Kyla said. "After that, get dressed because the bus is coming soon."

Back in his room, Jay found 2X looking at his outer space posters. "Please tell me about these pictures," she said.

Jay grinned. He'd finally met someone who wanted to hear everything he knew about outer space – someone who wouldn't roll their eyes at him or run off when he talked about his favorite subject. This cyborg would listen to him all day and all night, if he could stay awake that long. He talked a long time about the Milky Way galaxy, the solar system, the Challenger Space Shuttle, Hubble, and was just starting on Mars ...

"Jay," Kyla yelled, "shake a leg!"

Jay shook his right leg and continued talking about Mars.

"Why are you moving your leg about?" 2X asked.

"Because my sister said to," Jay answered, pointing to Mars on the poster on his wall. "Then I have to go to school."

A few minutes later, Kyla banged on his door. "Are you dressed yet? I hope you're wearing shorts and sandals, because it's hot outside."

Jay grabbed his shorts and sandals and quickly put them on.

"Jay," 2X asked, "may I play with your toys today while you are gone?" She looked longingly at his bins of toys. "Until now, I have only seen pictures of Earth-toys. I very much want to use them."

Jay nodded and pulled down his army and McDonald's figures. "You can play with these," he said generously, putting the bins on the floor. "When I get back, I'll tell you more about our solar system."

"Thank you," 2X said. "I want to listen to you for many hours, many days and months about the Earth's solar system."

"Jay!" Kyla screamed, "the bus is coming down the street. Hurry up!"

Kyla was waiting at the bottom of the stairs ready to throw his backpack and lunch into his arms. He was almost out the door when Kyla stopped him. "Why didn't you put a shirt on?"

Jay kept running. "Because you said to put on my shorts and sandals," he yelled over his shoulder.

Kyla ran after him and grabbed his arm. "You can't

go to school like that." Go put a t-shirt on. And thanks a lot. Now you'll miss the bus and I'll have to drive you to school and be late for first period."

Jay scratched his ear. He didn't understand why she was thanking him, but to be polite, he said, "You're welcome."

Chapter Four

2X MEETS KYLA

Jay was glad Mrs. Kim was back at school, but even so the day didn't go well for him. All he could think about was 2X. He frowned at the clock all day, waiting for it to turn 3:30. He felt bad that Mrs. Kim had to keep telling him to get back to work.

"Finally!" he said out loud when it was time to go. He could hardly wait to go home to 2X.

He was in the bus line when he saw Kyla walking up to him.

"Jay," she said, "I decided to pick you up so we can stop at the store. That way we won't have to stop practicing volleyball to go later."

"No," he told her. "I want to go home now. I want to see 2X."

Kyla rolled her eyes. "Look, there's no so such thing as this 2X. And even if there was, you'd see her sooner by going with me, I promise you."

Slowly, Jay got in the car and started rubbing his forehead. Frowning at the clock all day had given him a headache.

As soon as they were home, Kyla said, "Jay, what's that noise?"

"It's probably 2X," he answered, heading toward the stairs.

"No, probably your radio – that means you left it on all day. Go turn it off." She put a package of popcorn in the microwave and started the oven.

"Oh, first you need to call Mom."

Jay speed dialed Mom and said, "Mom, I don't want to talk – I want to play with 2X." Then he hung up and raced Noodle upstairs. Jay opened his door and saw 2X on the floor with one of his McDonald's toys. It was a plastic Big Mac with arms and legs. She was crashing into it with his army tank.

"What are you doing?" Jay asked.

2X looked up. "I'm making a Mac attack. Dr. Eo said Earth-people have millions of them."

Jay knelt down beside her. "I don't think that's what it means. I'll ask Kyla."

Jay found Kyla in the kitchen putting his popcorn on the table.

"Was it your radio?" she asked.

"No," Jay said, taking the popcorn from her. "It was 2X, and she wants to know what a Mac attack is."

Kyla laughed and ruffled Jay's hair. "You crack me up."

"Tell me about a Mac attack," Jay said, backing away.

"Okay." It means someone really wants a Big Mac," Kyla laughed again. "Ask 2X if they have McDonald's on her planet."

"Sure," Jay said, running back upstairs. The second he was in his room, he began explaining the Mac attack. He stopped when he saw 2X sitting by his window with her eyes closed.

He tiptoed over. "Are you asleep?"

2X touched her wire hair, but didn't open her eyes. "I am receiving the next file for the Ready for More English program," she said. "Place your ear close to my hair. You will hear it coming from Zuse."

As Jay leaned close, he heard soft taps – some long, some short. It reminded him of the Morse code machine he'd seen at the Museum of American History on a field trip last year.

Then he heard another sound. "I think your stomach is growling again," he said.

2X opened her eyes and said to her computer, "Off." To Jay, she said, "I need to put food in my stomach again. It is much trouble to have a stomach."

Jay found an old golf ball in his closet and gave it to her. "Here," he said, "it's white like Captain Quasar's head."

2X took a bite and chewed. Little bits of white plastic stuck in her teeth.

To drown out the sound of her crunching, Jay put his hands over his ears until she finished chewing.

"Jay," Kyla yelled from downstairs, "time to practice."

"I have to help Kyla with volleyball," he explained. He pointed to the window facing the backyard. "I'll be down there." Noodle followed him.

"Do you have water in your house?" 2X asked, spitting more golf ball shell into Jay's wastepaper basket. "I wish to give my teeth a bath."

Jay pointed to the bathroom he shared with Kyla.

"Turn on the faucet," he said. "You can use my cup – it's the one with Mars on it."

On the lawn, Kyla practiced spiking the ball over the net.

"You're getting good," Jay told her, tossing the ball back to her.

"Thanks, but I'm no good at getting them. If only you could spike them to me." Jay felt like someone had hit him in the stomach. He wished he was good at sports, but sometimes his brain, arms and legs refused to work together, especially in group games. Then he remembered he was a strong swimmer and felt better. Just last summer he'd helped his team win the city all-neighborhood meet in the hundred-yard relay race.

He threw the ball over the net again and waited for Kyla to slam it back.

"Jay," she suddenly screeched, dropping the ball. She pointed to his bedroom window. "There's something in your room!"

Jay looked up, shading his eyes from the sun. "That's 2X," he said, "she's from planet Zuse, which is five million light years away from us, and her hair receives programs from …"

"Stop!" Kyla screamed. "It's a space alien? Don't you care there's a space alien in your bedroom?"

Jay flapped. "Yes, I care a lot. 2X is funny, and she wants to hear everything about the solar system."

"Well I'm in charge of you, and I'm getting rid of it!" Kyla yelled.

Jay and Noodle followed Kyla to his room. "2X," he said, "this is my sister. Kyla, this is my friend, 2X." He was proud that he'd remembered the rule about introducing people.

2X put out her hand, but Kyla swung hers behind her back, refusing to be properly introduced.

"That's rude," Jay told his sister. "The rule is, when someone puts out her hand, you're supposed to shake it." He smiled because now he'd remembered two manners in a row. Manners were hard for him.

Kyla pointed to 2X's face. "What's that blue stuff around your eyes? Did you get into my new eye shadow?"

"Thank you for leaving your eye shadow in the water room," 2X replied. "I read that Earth-people leave items in their water rooms for all to use, such as soap, towels, toilet paper and nose tissues." Then she looked at her eyes in the mirror. "I will write about this in my social studies report when I return to Zuse."

Kyla marched over to 2X. "I don't know who you are, but I'm telling you to S-P-L-I-T!"

"One minute, please, Sister Kyla," 2X said, turning on her computer. "Split!" she said into it.

"Many definitions," a kid voice said. "*Split* can mean: to rip, to share, or to leave quickly."

Kyla covered her face and moaned. "Ohhhhh, just what I need – another Jay."

2X touched Kyla's arm and asked, "Sister Kyla, please explain how I can be Jay? I am 2X."

During all this Jay sat quietly on the floor watching them. Finally, he said, "2X, sometimes I don't understand her either."

Kyla threw herself down on Jay's bed and pounded the pillow, "I just can't win."

2X and Jay patted Kyla's back. "Do you mean you can't win a volleyball game?" Jay asked. "First, you have to make the team."

Kyla jumped off the bed and screamed at 2X, "You're too much, you stupid creature. Get out of here right now! I can't take any more weirdos around here."

"No!" Jay yelled, flapping hard. "Call Mom at work and get permission for her to stay. 2X is my friend. Then he added, "Her name is not Too Much, it's 2X."

Kyla thought for a minute, then a smile spread

across her face. "You call Mom," she said. "Tell her there's an alien in your room, and ask if it is okay for her to stay 'til she and Dad get home." Then she went to get the cordless phone and tossed it to Jay.

Jay pressed the speaker button and held the phone out so Kyla and 2X could both hear. He told Mom everything.

"Jay, Sweetie," Mom said, "this is your first imaginary friend. Of course, she can stay."

"Mom!" Kyla yelled into the phone, "there really is a space alien," but Mom had already hung up. She shook her head and said, "You're going to be sorry, Mom."

After Kyla left, Jay took down his bin of space toys. He and 2X spent the rest of the afternoon lining up his space sets all over his room. He had never been this happy in his life.

Chapter Five

When Kyla heard her parents' car in the driveway, she ran outside and screamed, "Mom, Dad, there's a space alien in Jay's room!" Then the three of them rushed upstairs.

As they entered Jay's room, Jay and 2X were lining up the last of his space toys on the floor.

When Mom saw 2X, she gasped. Dad led her over to Jay's bed where they both sat down.

2X put out her hand. "It is nice to meet you, Mother and Father," she said. She offered her hand to Mom first.

Mom didn't say a word. She just sat and stared at her.

Jay took his mom's hand and put it in 2X's. "It's polite to shake hands," he reminded her.

Dad got up and walked all around 2X. "It's hard to believe, but I think you really are a space alien. Are you a robot?"

"Actually, Father," 2X explained, "I am a cyborg. I have some mechanical parts and some human parts. For example, I have a stomach in here," she said, pointing to her middle. Then she showed Mom and Dad her computer arm. "My computer is like your Earth-brain. It controls everything I do. I have many programs in my computer." Then she turned it on and demonstrated her new English program.

"Dad," Kyla said, "she probably brought horrible germs from Zuse. You should get rid of her now."

Dad put up his hand. "Hold on, Kyla, she looks clean and healthy to me."

But Kyla didn't give up. "Mom," she yelled. "You do something. Nobody I know has a space alien in their house. What if my friends see her?"

After this introduction, Jay and his family went to the kitchen to talk about 2X.

"I think we should contact her parents," Mom suggested.

Dad was at the counter making hamburger patties. "Good idea," he said. "Jay, go upstairs and ask 2X how we can talk to her parents."

"I do not have parents," 2X called down. She had been listening quietly from the top of the stairs. "Scientists made me. Do you want to talk to Dr. Eo? He programs me."

Mom and Dad looked up, surprised.

"2X, please come down here," Mom called.

2X took the stairs three at a time and sat down next to Jay. Then she spoke into her arm, "Dr. Eo, Mother and Father want to talk with you."

Jay pointed to 2X's arm. "You can talk into her computer," he explained.

"Dr. Eo," Mom asked, "What should we feed 2X? When is her bedtime? Is there anything that upsets her?"

"I installed a stomach in her just before she went to Earth," Dr. Eo said. "I believe she can digest any Earth-food. She will go to bed when your son does. She is programmed to lower her eye covers and to shut down most of her power then, but she does not sleep like Earth-children. For example, she does not dream or snore. She gets upset when she gets too many commands at once. You will notice her shutting down briefly. Just remind her to reboot herself and she will be fine."

"Dr. Eo," Dad asked, putting his head close to 2X's arm, "what should we do if she gets sick? Where should she stay when my wife and I are at work and the kids are at school?"

2X's computer crackled a little and Dr. Eo answered. "Cyborgs do not get sick, but if she should malfunction, please contact me. I will beam down the proper corrections. 2X would love to go to Earth-school, but if you cannot enroll her, she has a self-care program to use when you are gone. She can amuse herself at home with books, watching television or videos, using a computer and playing with Jay's toys. Or you can teach her to do household chores."

One more thing: 2X has much curiosity about Earth. We scientists do not know how she got this curiosity since our other cyborgs have none. But she has begged us to let her visit Earth ever since we manufactured her, so I am asking you to let her stay with you for one Earth-year."

Kyla, 2X and Jay watched as Mom and Dad whispered together.

"Dr. Eo," Mom spoke into 2X's arm, "we will let 2X stay on a trial basis for two weeks. That way, we'll know if she fits into our family. A year's a long time, you know. Can her stomach digest regular human food? Do I need to go to a special grocery store for her?"

"I am almost certain she can digest all Earth-food," Dr. Eo answered. "Please contact me if her stomach or any other part of her malfunctions. Thank you for hosting her for two weeks. That is all."

Hearing this, Jay jumped up and down singing, "2X can stay, can stay, can stay." Then he went over to the pantry, found his oatmeal crackers and shared them with her.

But Kyla wasn't happy. "I don't believe this! You're letting a space alien stay in our house," she said.

"Yes," Dad answered. She's a built-in friend for Jay. What more could we ask?"

"You're letting that crazy cyborg stay because she's a friend for Jay," Kyla yelled. "What about me? I don't want her."

Mom patted Kyla's arm. "Honey," she said, "you have lots of friends, friends who understand you. You know how hard it is for Jay to find friends like that."

Leaving the kitchen, Kyla yelled, "Well, I won't have any friends once they see her!"

"Kyla," Dad called after her, "2X will be part of the family for the next two weeks, starting now – at 7:30 p.m. I expect you to be kind to her, and to teach her how to do some chores around the house."

Only Jay heard Kyla say under her breath, "I'll teach her all right!" He was happy, thinking that meant she would do a good job teaching 2X.

The next day before Jay and Kyla left for school, Kyla smiled slyly as she told 2X to let Noodle out during the day whenever he barked by the door. Something about her reminded Jay of the fox in his reader. He scratched his ear thinking. "Their smile's the same, the same," he said out loud, pleased with himself.

At school, Jay had to remind himself a million times to pay attention and to finish his papers. All he wanted to think about was 2X and what he'd tell her about outer space as soon as he got home. Should he start with N.A.S.A. – the National Aeronautic Space Administration, the National Air and Space Museum or his favorite planet, Saturn?

When Jay got home, he was surprised that Noodle didn't come to meet him. He ran around the house calling, "Noodle, Noodle!"

Jay found Kyla in the kitchen. "Where's Noodle?" he asked.

"Don't know," she answered, "maybe he's hiding somewhere."

Jay went to his room to ask 2X about Noodle. She was reading his book on black holes.

"When you were at school," she told him, "Noodle barked by the door when a man put some paper items in the receptacle outside the front door. I remembered that Kyla told me to let him out the door when he barks, so I opened the door for him. I saw that he goes very fast on his four legs. I am going to ask the scientists to manufacture two more legs for me."

Kyla overheard the conversation and ran upstairs. "2X," she said, "that was totally stupid! You were supposed to let Noodle out the *back* door. Our backyard is fenced so he can't run away."

"Sister Kyla," 2X asked, "instruct me in the ways of finding Noodle, and I will do so."

But Kyla waved her hand and said, "You won't find him. I'm afraid it's *adios*, Noodle."

At dinner that night, Kyla told Mom and Dad that 2X had let Noodle out the front door.

Jay started to cry.

"Son," Dad said, "let's go look for Noodle right now – it's still light outside. Oh, and bring his leash in case we find him."

"As they were leaving, Kyla said, "Jay, I'll make lost-dog signs – in case you don't find him. We can put them around the neighborhood tomorrow morning. Good luck, you two!"

The next morning before school, Jay and Kyla were getting ready to put the signs up. 2X said, "Sister Kyla, my stomach is growling. I would like to have the white liquid you call milk. May I put some in a cup and warm it in that machine when you are gone?" She pointed to the microwave oven.

Kyla pushed her fist in the air and said, "Sure, give the milk twenty."

Then she left with Jay to put the signs on telephone poles around the neighborhood, looking for Noodle at the same time. They didn't find him. Jay cried and flapped all the way home, but they had to get ready for school.

When they got back, 2X was standing in front of the microwave, fanning big clouds of smoke.

Jay started running around the kitchen yelling, "Fire, fire, fire!"

In the meantime, Kyla punched the off button and looked through the little microwave window. "It's not on fire," she said, breathing hard. "2X, you burned the milk, the mug, everything! How much time did you give it?"

Pointing to the microwave pad, 2X said, "I touched the numbers, two and zero enough times to make twenty minutes," she said.

"Dummy," Kyla yelled, "you were supposed to give it twenty *seconds*, not twenty *minutes!*"

"I am quite sorry, Sister Kyla, I will remove the black parts in the microwave oven now," 2X said.

"Don't bother," Kyla answered. "You ruined it, and my parents will have to get a new one. They're going to be sooo mad at you."

That night Kyla told Mom and Dad about the microwave. After exchanging worried looks with Mom, Dad put a cup of water in the microwave and gave it thirty seconds. "It seems okay," he said with relief, "but I think I'd better give 2X microwave lessons."

"Dad," Jay said, "I want to look for Noodle now."

Dad shook his head. "I think we better call the pound. Maybe somebody him and took him there."

"I'll get the phone number," Mom said, getting up.

Dad called the pound but Noodle wasn't there.

Jay started to cry, "Want Noodle, want Noodle."

"Let's put a lost-dog ad in the *Washington Post*," Mom said, taking the newspaper from the counter. She called the *Post* and placed the ad. "Jay," she said, "the ad lady said, 'I hope you find Noodle. Lots of people find their pets through our ads.'"

As Dad gave 2X her microwave lesson, Jay and Mom loaded the dishwasher. Jay enjoyed placing and replacing the plates and bowls so they'd all fit. It helped to take his mind off Noodle.

The next day before Kyla and Jay went to school, Kyla told 2X to do some chores: sort and put away the clothes in the dryer and vacuum the bedrooms.

After school, Kyla made Jay's popcorn as usual, and then inspected all the bedrooms. When she got to Jay's room, she found 2X and Jay sitting at his computer pointing at photos of Saturn's rings.

"2X, you did a nice job vacuuming the bedrooms," Kyla praised her.

"Thank you, Sister Kyla," 2X said, sharing Jay's popcorn.

When it was time for Kyla's volleyball practice, 2X followed Jay and Kyla to the backyard. As Jay threw the volleyball over and over for Kyla to spike back, 2X sat against the fence to watch.

After a half an hour Jay shook his arm and said, "My arm is getting tired. I want to stop."

"So who's going to help me practice, 2X?" Kyla asked.

"That is a good idea," 2X answered, and walked over to Jay's side of the net.

Kyla rolled her eyes. "Give me a break," she said, glaring at 2X.

2X typed "break" into her computer, read the screen and then set a tiny dial on her shoulder. Her arm made a whirring sound as it spun around and slammed the ball. She slammed it so hard it burst into shreds.

Kyla's mouth fell open as she stared down at the shreds. Then she went inside and came back with another ball. "This time," she said, "don't hit it so hard."

Jay cheered his sister as she began to retrieve and hit the balls 2X sent flying over the net. "I bet you're going to make the team," he told her.

Kyla caught her breath and said, "If 2X and I practice every day till the tryouts, I will for sure!"

When Kyla was too tired to practice any more, 2X and Jay went to the family room. 2X started a *Star Wars* video while Jay picked up the phone to check for messages about Noodle. Not a single person had called. He found Kyla on her bed. "Kyla," he said, "No one's called about Noodle. Maybe the signs came down. Could you go check?"

Kyla rolled off her bed and put on her sneakers. "Okay," she said, taking a CD from her dresser. "I need to return this to Heather. I'll do it after I check the sign near her house."

Jay went back to the family room to watch *Star Wars* with 2X. Maybe it would help him stop worrying about Noodle.

Chapter Six

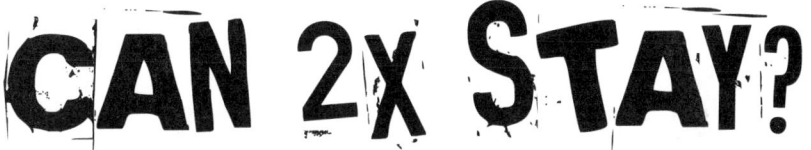

After dinner that night Mom and Dad called a family meeting. "2X," Mom said, "you wait in Jay's room while we talk. This time with the door closed, please."

Mom sat twisting her hands, "Things aren't going well around here. 2X almost ruined the microwave – in fact, she could've set the house on fire. Today she vacuumed and some of my underwear is missing, plus the vacuum's broken, and ..."

Kyla jumped out of her seat, "That's not all, Mom. 2X wrecked my new eye shadow." Then she slapped her forehead and got a funny look on her face.

"What is it, Honey?" Mom asked.

"Er, nothing," Kyla answered.

"I agree, Dad said, "I think we have to send 2X back to Zuse. She's a sweet cyborg, but this isn't working out."

Jay started flapping and yelled, "No! 2X is my friend." Then he flung himself on Mom's lap and cried, "Noodle's gone, 2X is going. Everything's bad, everything's bad."

Dad sighed and rubbed the back of his neck as he always did when he was thinking.

Suddenly Kyla jumped up and said, "I need to go to Heather's for a few minutes. I'll be right back."

Jay was still crying as he and 2X wiped the counters after they had done the dishes. Suddenly he heard the front door open and a dog's excited bark.

"Noodle?" he hollered, tearing into the front room.

As soon as he got near, Noodle jumped from Kyla's arms and started pawing Jay's leg. Delighted, Jay picked him up and rubbed his cheek on the dachshund's smooth brown back.

Hearing all the noise, Mom, Dad and 2X came running. "How did you find him?" Dad asked.

At first Kyla didn't say anything. "It's a long story," she finally said.

"Let's hear it in the family room," Dad said.

When they were all gathered, Kyla sat down on the ottoman near Jay. "It's like this," she started, biting her lip. "When 2X came, everything changed. Jay, you started liking 2X more than me, and 2X, you wrecked my eye shadow and played with Jay every minute of the day. And Mom and Dad, I could tell you wanted me to be like 2X and do chores all the time, and ..."

"Sister Kyla," 2X interrupted, touching Kyla's arm, "I'm sorry for doing chores and for wrecking your eye shadow."

"I know," Kyla said, "and I forgive you. But there's something I want you to forgive *me* for – something huge." She turned away for a few seconds. "I didn't teach you how to do your chores right on purpose. I wanted you to mess up so Mom and Dad would send you back to Zuse – the sooner the better. Like, I knew Noodle would bark at the front door when the mailman came and that you'd let him out. I wanted Mom and Dad to think he was lost and that it was all your fault. Heather had e-mailed me when I got up that morning to say she had a cold and was staying home. I phoned her right back and told her that you might let Noodle out the front door and asked her to watch for him as she passed her house. Then I asked her to bring Noodle in and keep him at her house for a few days."

Jay turned to his sister. "Did Heather find Noodle? Why didn't you tell her to bring him back when she found him?"

Kyla gave Jay a hug. "That's what I love about you," she said. "You don't see the bad things in people."

"Yes I do," Jay said, pointing to her face. "I can see every one of your zits."

Kyla looked at the ceiling and blew her bangs. "On the other hand, that's what I *don't* like about you – you say exactly what you're thinking."

Jay flapped a little and asked, "Well, do you like me or not?"

Kyla studied his face and said, "I love you, Little Dork. You drive me crazy, but I love you. I'll even love you when you're a big, grown-up dork."

After a slight pause Dad said, "Kyla, that was a terribly mean and dishonest thing you did, making it look like 2X let the dog run away and teaching her to do her chores wrong. For your punishment, you're not to visit, talk to or email your friends for two weeks."

"But Dad," Kyla yelled, "they'll think I'm mad at them or something."

"Then you can email them – once – and let them know."

"Mom, Dad," Jay blurted, pulling them towards the back door. "Come see how Kyla can get spiked balls and spike them back. 2X and I helped her learn how."

Mom put her arm around Kyla and Jay's shoulders as they walked outside. "Kyla," she said, "I'm not happy about what you did, but I am glad you can be so honest with your feelings toward your brother. You've learned an important lesson – there are negative parts to your brother's Asperger's as well as positive ones.

Dad picked up the volleyball and threw it to 2X. "There are good and bad parts to everyone," he added, "and part of growing up is learning to accept that."

"2X," Jay asked, "do you have any bad parts?"

2X pointed to her stomach. "I believe my stomach is a bad part," she said. "It growls, and I must put food in it many times each day."

"No, 2X," Jay said, "stomachs are good, and right now my stomach wants ice cream."

Mom laughed and asked, "Who wants to go inside and have sundaes?"

Everyone helped get the ice cream, chocolate sauce, candy sprinkles, whipped cream, bowls and spoons ready.

Jay saw Mom and Dad whispering again.

Then Dad looked at Kyla and Jay and said, "If you two don't have a lot of homework this weekend, Mom and I were thinking we could all go camping – some place close by."

"I don't have much," Kyla said. "Could we bring the volleyball net?"

Dad nodded.

Jay started to flap. "I just remembered. "I have to do my report. It's due on Monday. It's about an Aesop fable." He covered his ears and shut his eyes as everyone groaned.

"Jay," Mom asked, "how long have you had to do this report?"

Jay looked at his feet and said, "A month, I think."

"Have you read the fable?" Dad asked.

"Yes, and Mrs. Kim gave us a rubric to use. I think I can do it on Saturday."

"If you work hard and get it done," Dad told him, "we can watch movies that night – you can pick them and I'll make my famous root beer floats and popcorn. We'll go camping some other time when we have the whole weekend."

Mom put her hand on Jay's shoulder. "You know we're here to help if you need it."

"I know," Jay said, flapping a little. "It's just a lot of work."

Chapter Seven

That weekend, Jay and 2X worked on his report. First he read Aesop's fable *The Fox and the Grapes* to 2X. Afterwards he explained, "It means the fox wanted the grapes, but when he couldn't reach them, he said they were sour. He didn't know that since he didn't eat any, but he was angry, so he said they were sour." Then he read the fable rubric to her. "I'll make the diorama choice," he told her. "Can you go ask Mom for an empty shoe box?"

While 2X was gone, Jay found markers, glue and construction paper in his desk.

He decided to make a stand-up fox and a grapevine.

He drew an outline of an angry-looking fox with his arm reaching up. Then he drew a grapevine that was taller than the fox's arm. He was ready to draw the details when 2X came back with a shoe box. She sat on the floor to keep him company.

"Now for the hard part," he told her – writing the report."

Just then Mom passed by Jay's room with a basket of laundry. "How's your report going?"

Jay giggled, "It isn't going anywhere – it's right here. He knew she was really asking how much he had done.

Mom put the basket down and looked over the rubric. "Do you understand what you have to do?"

"Yes," Jay said, flapping a little. "I have to write at least two sentences for each question here – in paragraphs. Then I have to practice reading the report."

Mom grinned and told him, "You're one smart cookie."

Jay glanced at 2X and explained, "It means I'm smart."

2X put her hand on Mom's shoulder. "Mother," she asked, "Do you think that I am a smart cookie, too?"

Mom grinned at her. "Yes I do, 2X."

2X read Jay's Saturn book while he typed the ten answers for his report. He stopped four times. Once to use the bathroom, twice to get a snack and once to sit and click his light-up pen

"Brother Jay, why do you turn that little light on and off?" 2X asked him.

Jay kept his eyes on the blinking light and said, "Can't explain – it just helps me," he said.

When Jay finished the report, he found Mom cleaning his sink. "I got it done," he told her.

"Nice job. You can read it to me now." She sat down on the edge of the tub and listened.

"Jay, did the rubric tell you what to do while reading your report?"

Jay scratched his head. "Oh yeah," he said, "I'm supposed to keep my place with my finger, raise and lower my voice and look at the audience sometimes."

Back in his room, Jay flicked his fingers and said, "How am I supposed to remember all that stuff?"

"I know it's hard," Mom agreed. "Look up the rubric, then read it to me again. I'm going to get some coffee."

"It is a lot to remember," 2X told him. I must give my big report about Earth-children when I go back to Zuse, so each day I transmit observations to Dr. Eo. He is recording my transmissions for me. Otherwise, I would never remember all that I observe here."

Jay bounced in his chair. "2X, you just gave me an idea. Can you transmit to me through my headset?"

"I think I can," she said. "I will try. You stay here, and I will try to transmit from the kitchen."

Soon Jay heard 2X close the kitchen door, "What should I say?"

"It works!" Jay said, running down to his mom.

"Mom, when I wear my headset, 2X can help me. Can she come to school with me tomorrow?"

Mom put down her coffee mug. "Back up a little. I was reading the paper and wasn't paying attention to what you and 2X were doing just now."

Jay took two small steps backwards.

2X did too. "Brother Jay," she asked, "is this the Earth-game called 'Follow the Leader'?"

Mom smiled and said, "'Back up a little' means I want Jay to explain what made him ask me if you can go to school with him."

Jay flapped. Everything was clear to him. Why did he have to stop and explain it? "2X just reminded me to do all the stuff I'm supposed to remember for my report," he said. "She transmitted from the kitchen to my room – that means she can do it from the hall outside my classroom tomorrow – if you let her go to school with me."

"Hold on," Mom said, going upstairs, "I need to talk to your sister."

Jay knew "hold on" meant "wait," not for him to grab onto something. He had to wait for Mom to go upstairs, talk to Kyla and come back down. Then she'd tell him if 2X could go to school with him.

Mom returned a few minutes later. "I just talked to

Kyla. She said she'll pick up 2X, take her to your school, then bring the two of you home."

Kyla came running down the stairs. "Mom," she said, "what if the school has a no-cyborg policy?"

Mom slapped her forehead. "You're right! I should've thought of that. I'll call Mrs. Marks first thing tomorrow morning. I'll tell her you'll stay with 2X the whole time she's in the building."

Kyla turned to Jay. "You owe me big time for this. You and 2X can help me with my spiking today – and it won't count toward your library time, either."

"That's not fair!" Jay said. "I need a book on Hubble."

"Tough cookies," Kyla told him. Then she took 2X's hand and said, "Come with me and I'll find some school clothes for you. I think I have some things that are small enough for you."

Jay watched as his sister took 2X upstairs to her room. He thought 2X's Zuse outfit looked very comfortable. Why would she want to wear anything else?

Early next morning, Jay heard Mom talking on the phone. "Yes, Mrs. Marks, my daughter Kyla will bring 2X at 2:30 when the report begins. Then she'll take Jay and 2X home after he's given his report."

Jay jumped out of bed and tapped 2X on the back. The tiny red light in her neck was on. That meant she was still on her "rest" program. He'd have to wait until it changed to green before he could talk to her. He sat on her bed and watched the tiny light for a while. A little later, the light switched to green indicating that she was "awake," so Jay told her the good news.

At breakfast Kyla reminded Jay and 2X, "I need you to help with volleyball as soon as I pick you up from school this afternoon, okay?"

"I will be honored to help you, Sister Kyla," 2X answered.

"Sure," Jay added, making lines of sugar on his oatmeal.

Jay couldn't help worrying about his report on the bus ride to school. What if Kyla forgot to pick up 2X? What if that sub was back and he wouldn't let him wear his headset? He took his report out of his back pack. Maybe practicing it would make him feel better.

"Is Foxie getting ready for his boring report?" Hunter teased.

The kid next to him laughed. Hunter went on, this time making his voice stay on exactly the same note. "Hello. My name is Jay. I am going to talk about the fox and the grapes. This report is so boring, it will put you to sleep." He closed his eyes and made a loud snoring noise. All the kids looked at Jay, then pretended to snore, too.

Jay looked out his window to distract himself. *I am going to give a great report*, he told himself.

Jay did his best to keep his leg from jiggling in class, but he kept remembering the way Hunter had teased him on the bus. He began to flap and hum. Mrs. Kim called him to her desk. "Jay, is something bothering you?" she asked.

"Yes," he answered, twisting the hem of his shirt, "my book report. I might mess up in front of the class."

Mrs. Kim glanced at her watch and said, "You have 10 minutes before your resource room time, but I think it's okay if you leave a little early. Ask Mr. Goodman to go over your report with you. I think it will help you relax."

Jay got his diorama and report and left.

"Can you help me?" Jay asked, entering the resource room.

"What's up, Jay?" Mr. Goodman asked.

Jay didn't look up at the ceiling because he knew the teacher was asking him what he needed help with.

Jay flapped a little, then put his diorama and report on Mr. Goodman's desk.

"Let's hear your report," he said, leaning back in his chair.

Jay took three slow deep breaths as he looked down at his report. He knew this was another way he could calm himself. As he read his report, he lost his place a few times, but remembered to keep glancing at Mr. Goodman for eye contact.

"What do you need to do to keep your place?" Mr. Goodman asked.

"Keep my finger under the sentence I'm reading," Jay answered, tapping his foot.

Jay finished reading his report. "Good job, Jay," he said. "You kept your place, you made eye contact and you remembered to raise and lower your voice." He gave him a high-five and added, "You're ready – you're going to do a fine job in class."

As Jay was returning to class, he met Kyla and 2X in the front hall outside the school office.

"I don't want to do this report," he told them.

"Just do your best," Kyla said. "I'll be right outside your classroom with 2X. As soon as you're done, we'll go home."

Jay took 2X's hand and they all walked down to his classroom. "Stay right here by the door," he told them. "2X, don't look through the window or the kids will see you and start yelling."

"Why will they yell?" 2X asked.

"They always yell when they see someone at the window," he said.

It was a little before 2:30 when Jay went inside. He put on his headset and waited for Mrs. Kim to start the reports. He had decided that if she asked for a volunteer to go first, he would raise his hand. He wanted to get it over with – and he knew he could go home right after it. He imagined himself with 2X on his computer hunting for more photos of Saturn.

Mrs. Kim asked for a volunteer to go first and called on Jay. He got up and walked to the front of the room with his report and diorama. Then he took a slow, deep breath and started to read.

"Remember to keep your finger under the sentence you are reading," he heard 2X tell him. He was already doing that. Next, 2X reminded him to raise and lower his voice. Jay did that in the middle of his sentence, and Hunter laughed.

Wrong time to change voice, Jay thought, but he went on.

"Hunter, that was rude," Mrs. Kim said.

Jay took another slow, deep breath and went on. Soon he heard 2X remind him to look at the audience. He didn't like looking at people's eyes, so he looked at their ears instead. Dad had told him once that ears and eyes were close enough on people's faces that looking at their ears was okay. As he looked around, he saw Mrs. Kim giving him the thumbs-up sign. He knew that meant he was doing a good job.

He read his last sentence and ran to his seat.

"Cool diorama," one kid said as the class clapped for him.

"Excellent job, Jay," Mrs. Kim said, walking over to him. She wrote a big "A" on his report.

Jay grinned at the "A." He had gotten many "A's" on his math papers, but this was his first for a report.

"Your turn, Hunter," Mrs. Kim.

"Um," Hunter mumbled, "I didn't finish it … um … because I had to go to my recital last night. My piano recital. I played a hard Beethoven song."

Jay looked back and forth at Hunter and Mrs. Kim. He noticed the class was dead quiet. What was happening?

"Song?" Mrs. Kim asked, making her eyebrows go way up.

Jay remembered that when adults do that, sometimes it meant they didn't believe you.

Jay watched as Hunter squirmed in his seat and his

face turned redder and redder. "Yeah," he answered, "I played Fur Eclipse – it was really hard."

Mrs. Kim walked over to Hunter's desk with her hand on her hip. "For some reason, Hunter," she said, "I'm not buying this. I'm calling your mother right after school to check this out."

Hunter put his head down on his desk and started to cry. "I didn't do it yet," he said between sobs, "it was too hard."

Jay looked at Hunter crying. *It wasn't too hard,* he thought – *not if you followed the rubric and practiced reading the answers.* He raised his hand. "Mrs. Kim," he said, "I could help Hunter with his report tomorrow during P.E."

"Me miss P.E.?" Hunter yelled, "no way!"

Mrs. Kim smiled again at Jay. "That's so kind of you, Jay," she said. "I'm sure Hunter would be glad to have the chance to erase his zero."

"Thanks, I guess," Hunter told Jay.

Just then Jay remembered he was supposed to leave right after his report. He whispered to Mrs. Kim to remind her. He took his diorama and report in his backpack and went out to meet 2X.

As they were getting in the car, Kyla saw the "A" on Jay's report. "Jay, this calls for a celebration. I'll treat you to something. What would you like?"

Jay buckled his seatbelt and said, "I'd like a book on Hubble."

"I'll get you one at the mall," Kyla said, starting the car.

2X's stomach growled. "Sister Kyla," she said, tapping her on the shoulder, "I need to put something in my mouth now."

"Okay," Kyla answered. "I can kill two birds with one stone at the mall."

"No!" Jay shouted. "You shouldn't kill birds. They're useful for the environment. They spread seeds and eat insects."

Kyla glanced at her brother in the rearview mirror. "Don't worry, Little Dork," she laughed, "I won't be killing any birds."

Jay thought a minute. Then he said, "You mean you can get me a book and food for Kyla by just going to the mall? That you don't have to go to two different places and park and stuff?"

"Right," Kyla answered.

"Thank you, Sister Kyla," 2X said. "Sometimes you are nice to me. I am going to miss you when I return to Zuse in eight days, seven hours and forty-five minutes."

"You're nice to me sometimes, too," Jay added. He noticed Kyla rolling her eyes in the mirror but he didn't know why.

"2X," Kyla said, "maybe you won't have to go back in eight days ... whatever the time you said. Remember Mom told Dr. Eo the two weeks was just a trial."

"That's right Kyla," Jay said, leaning towards his sister as far as his seatbelt would allow. "Maybe Mom and Dad will let her stay for a year."

Kyla turned her head back for a second. "I think it's in the bag, 2X. Mom's getting used to you sorting the wash, dusting and vacuuming. And I can teach you how to clean the toilets, wash the cars and iron my shirts."

Jay tapped Kyla on the shoulder and asked, "What does 'in the bag' mean?"

Kyla smiled in the mirror and said, "Means something is likely to happen."

2X bounced in her seat and turned to Jay. "I hope I can stay with you for a year. I am learning so much about Earth-Children at your house."

Jay turned to 2X. "I want you to stay with us forever. I want you to go to Groceries and More so I can show you the toy aisle where I found your capsule. I want you to go to school with me, to the Air and Space Museum and to my swim meets."

When the two weeks were up, Mom, Dad, Kyla, Jay and 2X gathered in the family room after dinner that night.

Mom cleared her throat, looked at 2X, and then at Jay. Jay couldn't tell from her face if she was going to say yes or no to 2X's staying on. He started to flap and hum.

"The thing is," Mom said looking around the room, "we have a small house and if 2X were here for a year, she should have her own room – we don't have an extra one."

"Mother," 2X said, "I do not need to have my own room. I do not have one on Zuse – only the scientists have their own rooms. As you can see, I didn't bring any of my possessions to Earth." She giggled and added, "I own nothing so small it would fit in the capsule with me."

"That's true," Dad said, turning to 2X. "You don't need a room with dressers and shelves. All you need is an outlet to recharge your battery and some place to rest, and we do have an extra bed."

"Well, we solved that problem," Kyla said smiling, pretending to slam a volleyball.

Mom frowned. "Then there's the problem of school. I called Mrs. Marks and she said she'd be delighted to have 2X at school, but she's worried about how a cyborg will do in a school of typical kids. Will she feel left out? Will she feel she's too different?"

Jay scooted next to Mom on the sofa. "Mom," he said, "I have Asperger's and nobody else does at my school – I am different but I do okay. So can 2X."

Mom and Dad smiled at each other and Mom kissed Jay on top of his head. "You do more than just okay," she told him, "everyone at school says you add a lot to your classes."

"Is that because he's a smart cookie?" 2X asked.

Mom, Dad and Kyla laughed.

"Yes," Mom answered hugging him, "but I think the main reason people like Jay is because he's Jay – he's honest, loyal, helpful, and ... well, all the things that make him who he is."

Jay got out of Mom's hug and asked, "Mom, Dad, does 2X get to stay for the year or not?"

Dad glanced at Mom, she nodded, and he said, "She can stay."

Mom added, "She can even start school tomorrow."

Kyla pushed her fist into the air and yelled, "Yes!"

2X and Jay ran around the room, yelling, "Yes! Yes! Yes!"

Jay stopped and took 2X's arm. "I'll call Dr. Eo," he said, pressing the button. "He needs to beam down some school programs ... because you're going to school with me tomorrow, tomorrow!"

Sayings and What They Mean

1. Take your seat. — Please sit down.

2. He's a space cadet. — He acts without thinking.

3. Nice of them to let me know. — It wasn't nice of them to let me know.

4. You're a pain in the neck. — You are bothering me now.

5. Keep your trap shut. — Do not talk now.

6. You didn't use your head. — You didn't think about what you did.

7. She's scarfing it down. — She's eating fast.

8. Third time's a charm. — The person hopes he'll be successful the third time.

9. It's raining cats and dogs. — It's raining very hard.

10. That's cool. — Can mean it's not very warm or it's something the person likes very much.

11. I just won the lottery.	Something amazing and unexpected just happened to me.
12. Shake a leg.	Hurry up.
13. Thanks a lot.	I am not happy or grateful for that.
14. I'm having a Mac attack.	I really want a Big Mac now.
15. Split.	Go away.
16. I just can't win.	No matter what I do, this situation is going to turn out badly for me.
17. You're too much.	You are hard for me to handle now.
18. Good luck.	I hope you get what you want.
19. Give me a break.	Tell me the truth, or Don't tell me that because I don't believe you.

If you have questions or would like to write the author, her email is: carolinelevine@gmail.net

APC

Autism Asperger Publishing Co.
P.O. Box 23173
Shawnee Mission, Kansas 66283-0173
www.asperger.net